OLIVIA™
Plays Soccer

adapted by Tina Gallo
based on the episode "Olivia and the Soccer Game"
written by Pat Resnick

illustrated by Jared Osterhold

Ready-to-Read

Simon Spotlight
New York   London   Toronto   Sydney   New Delhi

Based on the TV series OLIVIA™ as seen on Nickelodeon™

SIMON SPOTLIGHT
An imprint of Simon & Schuster Children's Publishing Division
1230 Avenue of the Americas, New York, New York 10020
OLIVIA™ Ian Falconer Ink Unlimited, Inc. and © 2013 Ian Falconer and Classic Media, LLC.
All rights reserved, including the right of reproduction in whole or in part in any form.
SIMON SPOTLIGHT, READY-TO-READ, and colophon are registered trademarks of Simon & Schuster, Inc.
For information about special discounts for bulk purchases, please contact Simon & Schuster Special Sales at
1-866-506-1949 or business@simonandschuster.com.
The Simon & Schuster Speakers Bureau can bring authors to your live event.
For more information or to book an event contact the Simon & Schuster Speakers Bureau at 1-866-248-3049
or visit our website at www.simonspeakers.com.
Manufactured in the United States of America 0313 LAK
First Edition 1 2 3 4 5 6 7 8 9 10
ISBN 978-1-4424-7248-8 (pbk)
ISBN 978-1-4424-7249-5 (hc)
ISBN 978-1-4424-7250-1 (eBook)

Mrs. Hoggenmuller gathered
all the girls together.
"It is almost time for our
first soccer game," she said.
"Come get your uniforms!"

Olivia smiled and said,
"I will be wearing
the red shirt!"

But Mrs. Hoggenmuller said,
"The red shirt is for the
goalie.
I have selected Francine
to be our goalie."

The next day Olivia tried on
her soccer uniform.
"Green is not my color,"
she said.

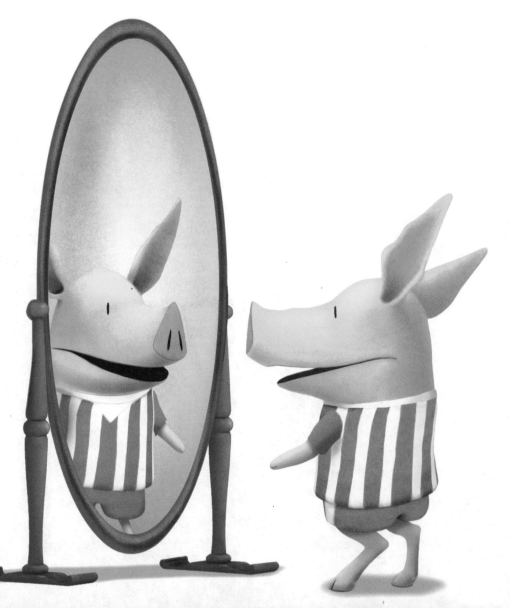

"It looks fine," Mother said.
"Green is the team color."

Olivia was not happy.
She tugged at her shirt.
"It is too big," she said.

"When you are part of a team, you need to look like the rest of the team," Mother replied.

Olivia decided to make her
own uniform.
She found a blue shirt and
shorts, and red bows for
her ears.

The next day was the game.
Olivia wore her own uniform.
But the other team was
wearing blue too!

"Olivia, you broke the rules," Mrs. Hoggenmuller said. "But since this is your first game, I will let you play."

Olivia took her place on the
field.
But her teammates got
confused and would not pass
the ball to her.

Francine was not a very
good goalie.
The blue team scored ten
goals.
The green team lost.

The team blamed Francine
for the loss.
"It was not all her fault,"
Olivia said.

"Maybe it was your fault!"
Francine said.
"Everyone thought
you were on the other team!"

Olivia was surprised
by what Francine said.

Back at home
Olivia tried on her uniform
again.
"I think your uniform is cool,"
Ian said.

The next day Olivia went to
the soccer field.
"My mother says I do not
have to be the goalie,"
Francine said.

"I will do it!"
Olivia shouted.

Francine was so happy!
Olivia was such a good
friend to volunteer!

Olivia the goalie got to wear
the red shirt.
And Olivia was a great goalie!

The green team won!
"I knew I would play better
with the right shirt,"
Olivia said.

That night Father tucked
Olivia in bed.

"Good night, my little goalie."

"Good night," Olivia said.